SAILOR

The Hangashore Newfoundland Dog

by Catherine Simpson
Illustrated by Joanne Snook-Hann

Tuckamore Books
a Creative Publishers imprint
St. John's, Newfoundland and Labrador
2008

Le Conseil des Arts | The Canada Council
du Canada | for the Arts

Appreciation is expressed to the Canadian Council for the Arts
for publication assistance.

We acknowledge the financial support of the Government of Canada
through the Book Publishing Industry Development Program
(BPIDP) for our publishing activities.

Illustrations © 1998, Joanne Snook-Hann
Printed on acid-free paper

Published by
TUCKAMORE BOOKS
an imprint of CREATIVE BOOK PUBLISHING
a Transcontinental Inc. associated company
P.O. Box 8660, St. John's, Newfoundland and Labrador A1B 3T7
First Printing November 1998
Second Printing August 1999
Third Printing February 2000
Fourth Printing July 2001
Fifth Printing May 2003
Sixth Printing October 2004
Seventh Printing August 2005
Eighth Printing February 2006
Ninth Printing February 2007
Tenth Printing December 2008
Printed in Canada by: TRANSCONTINENTAL INC.

National Library of Canada Cataloguing in Publication Data
Simpson, Catherine, 1953-
    Sailor
    ISBN 1-895387-98-1
I. Snook-Hann, Joanne. II. Title.
PS8587.I5453S35 1998   jC813'.54   C98-950258-9
PZ7.S6803Sa 1998

Tuckamore Books
a Creative Publishers imprint

To my personal heroes,
William and Jerry.
- C.S.

For my niece and nephew,
Stephanie and Jake.
- J.S.H.

Many thanks to Bosun, Cormack
and Dory, three beautiful
Newfoundland dogs who helped
make this book possible.

This is Sailor, a Newfoundland dog.
He lives with Ike and Ike's family in
Twillingate, Newfoundland.

Newfoundland dogs love to swim. But not too long ago, Sailor wasn't like other Newfoundland dogs. Sailor would not go in the water.

In the summer, when Ike and his friends went swimming in
the brook, Sailor would stay ashore.

In the fall, when Ike's family went berrypicking on the island, Sailor would stay ashore.

"Sailor, old buddy, you are a Newfoundland dog," said Ike. "Newfoundland dogs are famous for saving people from drowning. You should love to go in the water." Sailor just wagged his tail sadly.

Ike said, "Look at your fur. It's so thick and oily. It will keep you as warm as toast."

Sailor just whimpered.

Ike said, "Look at your toes. They're webbed, just like a duck's. You were born to swim."

Sailor just folded his paws.

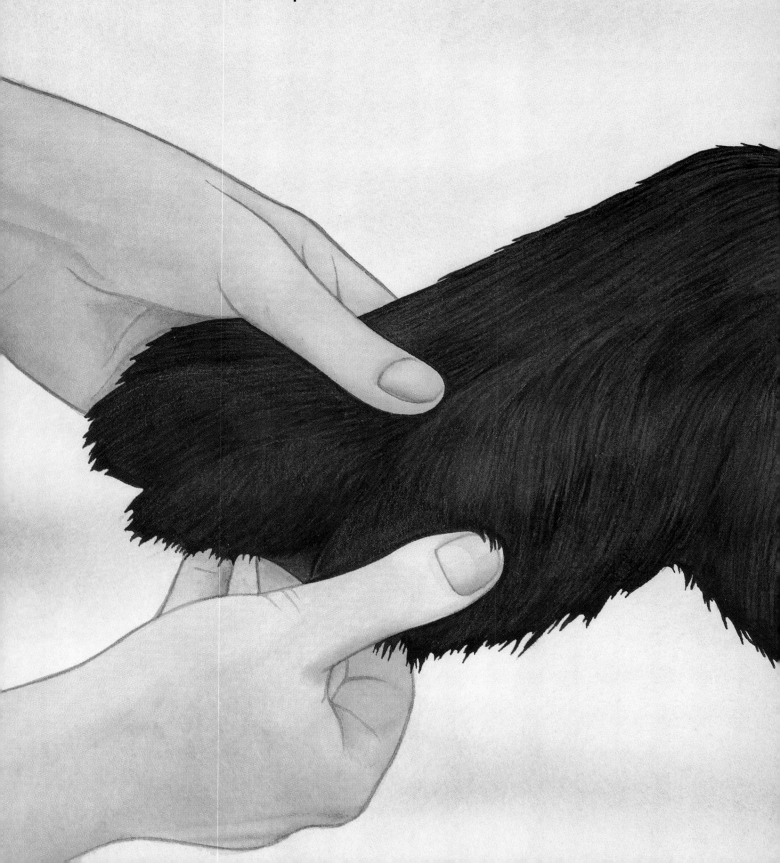

Ike said, "Look at the size of you! You're so big and strong. You could swim a mile in that water!"

Sailor just heaved a deep sigh.

Ike asked his parents what to do about Sailor. His dad, who was a teacher, said, "Maybe he just needs someone to teach him how to swim." His mom smiled and said, "Maybe he just needs a good reason to get in the water."

Ike thought about what his parents said. Maybe he could teach Sailor to like the water. "Come on, Sailor, old buddy," he said. "Let's play follow the leader!"

Sailor followed Ike to the beach. It was springtime, so the drift ice was piled on the shore in big ridges called ballycarters. Pans of ice dotted the salt water like flat white stepping stones.

Ike hopped from one pan to the next, trying to catch up to the older boys.

At first, the pans were close together, so it was easy to jump from one to the other. But then the wind began to blow. The slippery pans bobbed up and down on the waves, and floated farther and farther apart.

Ike came to a spot where he had to jump across wide open water, black and cold. It looked so far, but he jumped anyway.

His foot slipped.

He fell into the water!

It was ice cold. Ike struggled and splashed, but his boots filled with water and his clothes were as heavy as lead. It was so cold he could hardly breathe.

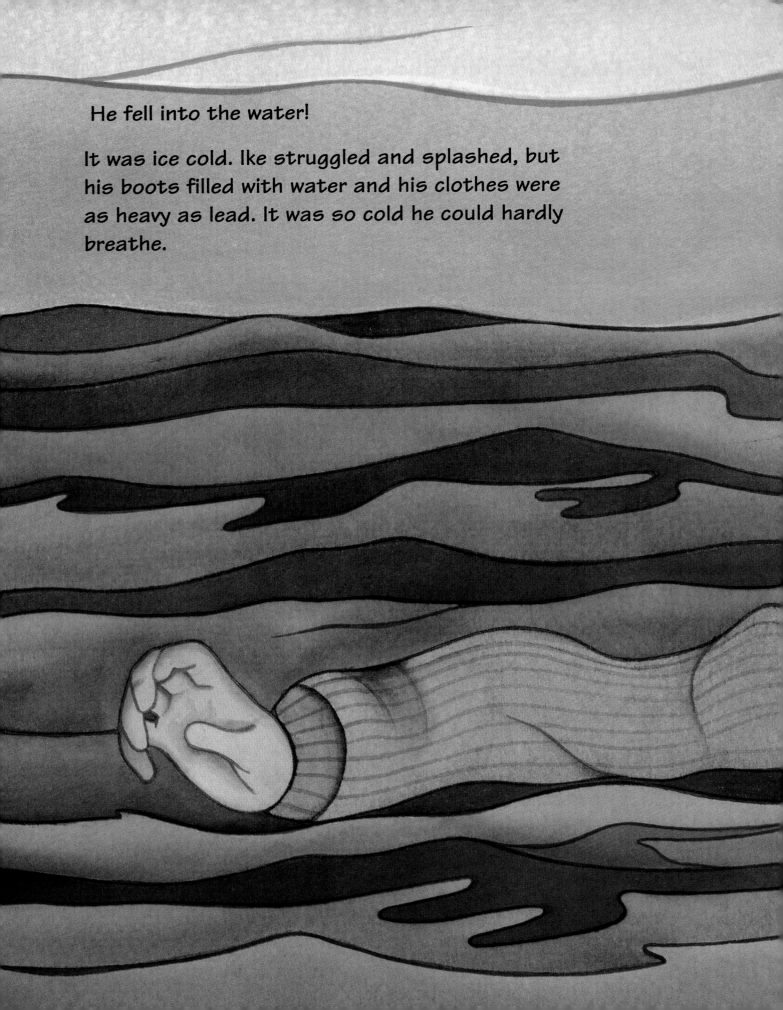

"Sailor! Help!" called Ike. "Help me!"

When Ike called out, a rare thing happened to Sailor. He jumped as if a lightning bolt had struck him. His head shot up and his tail shot out. He charged into that freezing water without a moments hesitation.

He shouldered his way through the ice pans. With powerful strokes of his huge paws, he churned through the water towards Ike.

Ike was gasping for breath and sinking, too cold to move a muscle. Sailor, with his great gentle jaws, grabbed his collar and dragged him up out of the water, on to an ice pan.

Ike lay in a heap, cold and wet, but safe.

Sailor lay down beside him and snuggled close to keep him warm until help came. The older boys, who saw it all, cheered and cried.

Later, Ike's dad said, "Ike my trout, your mom was right. That dog just needed a good reason to get in the water."

After that, no one ever called Sailor a hangashore anymore.

Now they call him a hero.